Uncliqueable

By Sydnie Boykins

DEDICATION

To **Mom** for your help with the title and plot when I got stuck, for editing this book for hours, and for encouraging me to continue writing.

To **Dad**, **Ciara, Chanel, Jamison,** and **Lauren** for always supporting me.

To **my grandparents** for inspiring us to follow our dreams.

To **Emmanuel** and **Alex** for reading this book and providing me with detailed feedback. I appreciate it a lot!
Thank you.

To my **readers**. I hope that this book inspires you to love, forgive, and to find the courage and confidence to always be **Uncliqueable.**

Table of Contents

LINDSAY

I wanted everyone to believe that I had friends. I decided to approach Rachel Edenbrooke in the hallway and ask to join her group for lunch, but I was scared. So I waited until I had a better chance to talk to her. Towards the middle of the day, I spotted her and her friend, Aaralyn Bridgeren, in the bathroom. Perfect.

Aaralyn had blonde hair and green eyes. She was pretty tall but slouched, so she looked like she was the same height as Rachel and I. She wore her hair in a messy side ponytail tied with a Klenden Country Day School ribbon. Oddly enough, Aaralyn never seemed to fully fit into

Rachel's group. The other girls didn't seem to like her much, but somehow Aaralyn made things work.

Rachel and I had a lot in common. We both wore our hair in a neat, high bun. We dressed alike (when we didn't have to be in dress code), and enjoyed wearing bracelets and hoop earrings. Her hair was only slightly darker than my own.

Rachel and Aaralyn both wore navy blue sweaters with the school emblem on them, the ones the popular kids wore.

Sometimes Rachel brought large bags of expensive chocolate candies from her house, put them in her pockets, and gave them out to classmates at random. I considered giving out candies too.

What am I doing? I thought. *I can't make it into their group*! I almost left the bathroom in fear. But I knew fear never got me anywhere before. Determination to fit in got the best of me, and I pushed all doubts aside.

After all, I had confidence; I just needed to be myself, the self that others didn't seem to like.

I interrupted Rachel and Aaralyn's conversation. "Rachel!" I said. Rachel jumped back from the mirror and turned to look at me when she heard my voice. I think I startled her. Instead of greeting me with a smile, she narrowed her eyes.

Rachel had never looked at me that way before, and I instantly wondered what caused her to make a face.

Aaralyn's eyes widened. I couldn't tell whether she was scared of Rachel or surprised that I dared to speak to Rachel. As much as I wanted to turn and run out of the bathroom, I decided against it. I remained in place and cleared my throat.

"Um," I said. "I know this is a little random, but do you mind if I sit with you guys at lunch today?"

Seconds of waiting for Rachel's response felt like minutes. I picked with the bracelet on my wrist. Even though the beads on it spelled out

"COURAGEOUS," I was anything but courageous. I was sweaty and shook all over.

Rachel narrowed her eyes even more. "Well, we-," she started to say, but Aaralyn cut her off.

"Rachel!" she said, and then backed down when Rachel glared at her.

"I...I just don't see why not, Rachel," Aaralyn finished in a quiet voice, as if intimidated.

Rachel looked me up and down; she looked at me like I was crazy.

I wondered what was going through her mind. After all, it wasn't like she was judging my clothes, right? We had the same school uniform: white polo shirts with the Klenden Country Day School emblem on them, khaki skirts, white knee socks, and tan boat shoes. Same as always. The one thing I did *not* have was a blue sweater.

Maybe I need to get a sweater. Ooh, maybe it's my bracelet. Rachel's bracelet doesn't spell out words; maybe she thinks that's too childish! My thoughts raced; I was desperate to know what had gone wrong. *Maybe it's my-*

"Sure," Rachel said, her voice hesitant. She didn't look at Aaralyn, as if to make me think she made her decision without Aaralyn's suggestion. "We sit at Table 4. See you there, I guess."

To me, those were magic words! Relief swept over me.

"Great!" I said. "Sounds great, guys! See you there!" I had tried making friends with the other girls in my grade before, but it hadn't worked. I figured that if I could make it into Rachel's group, I wouldn't have to worry about making friends anymore.

****

Lunch was interesting. For the first time, I felt like people actually listened to what I had to say! *Maybe I'm not boring after all?* I wondered.

I mean, I didn't really think I was boring. I just assumed other people thought I was. After all, my favorite hobbies were reading and writing.

Of course, I was the first one at the table. I didn't want to come late and miss out on the conversation. Rachel's other friends Mary, Tanner, and Brittany greeted me at Table 4. Rachel and Aaralyn didn't join until later.

Mary sat to my left. She was tall and had red hair. Tanner sat to Mary's left. She had chestnut brown hair and light brown eyes. They gave me a warm greeting.

Brittany sat on my right. She was black like me. You would think that we would have had something in common being the only black girls in our grade, but sometimes things don't work out the way you think they will. Let's just say that she didn't speak to me much.

She had dark brown hair that she wore in curls down her back. She said hi.

"Wait, so you write short stories?" Mary said after I shared the link to my blog with the girls. "That's awesome!"

I tried to gauge their interest to see if they were genuinely interested in what I had to say. It seemed like they were. Mary's smile *looked* genuine.

"Hey, I think Rachel's planning a spring break trip for us to go on if you want to g-!" Tanner said. But before she finished her sentence, Rachel and Aaralyn arrived and sat down at the opposite end of the table.

"Hey!" Rachel shouted, as if to capture everyone's attention. She put her tray down. Aaralyn had a timid smile on her face at first. She threw her tray down beside Rachel's.

Why was Aaralyn so hard to figure out? I still couldn't tell if she was scared of Rachel or not. Aaralyn looked at Rachel and rolled her eyes, as if to show me she didn't approve of Rachel's behavior. Yet she still hung out with her?

"Tanner, you were saying something about a spring break trip?" I tried to take the attention away from Rachel since no one else seemed to know how to.

Before Tanner could say anything, Rachel blurted out, "I'm just starting to plan our trip for break, and I don't have all the details yet!" She glared at Tanner.

"Right now, I'm thinking we should all go to Europe! Mary, Brittany, Tanner, Aaralyn, what do you think?"

Rachel didn't mention me.

Rachel really wanted to make a big deal of this trip that she intentionally didn't invite me on.

She could have at least asked me, I thought. The other girls didn't seem to care that Rachel had excluded me.

We started to eat, and Tanner, Mary, Brittany, and Rachel whispered to each other in hushed voices. Aaralyn was quiet. My face felt hot. I pretended that I didn't care that they weren't talking to me. I picked at my salad and buttered my breadstick. I pushed my rotini around my plate, wishing I had never asked to join Rachel's table.

Minutes passed and the girls continued talking. I focused on pushing the rotini onto the breadstick at the edge of my plate. I looked at the clock on the wall and wished lunch would end.

Finally, Rachel ended the conversation. "Lindsay," she said. "You're the new girl! You've gotta complete a dare! We've all been through one before!"

The other girls giggled, and even Aaralyn let out a tiny laugh. *Why are they laughing? Maybe they have some inside joke about me that I don't know about!*

My heart raced; I could see it pounding through my shirt.

I sank down in my seat. "What's the dare?" was all I managed to say.

They wanted me to walk to the center of the room and stand up on the random chair placed at the side of the salad bar.

At first I thought I didn't hear Rachel correctly. But I had.

"Wait...what?" I laughed. I shook my head. "That's ridiculous!"

"All of us have done it," Rachel said. "So now it's your turn if you want to sit here again!"

I knew for sure I didn't want to do it. *I can't. I*

won't let them make me look like an idiot, I thought. I never did anything I didn't want to in order to make people like me before. But I *didn't* want Rachel and her friends to make fun of me either.

Before I could open my mouth and acquiesce, one of our teachers walked over to the lunch tables and said, "9th graders, each table needs to pick one person to go to the kitchen, get a rag, and wipe down the table."

"Never mind the chair," Rachel whispered. "Why don't you get the *rag* instead, Lindsay?" The other girls didn't speak.

No, I wanted to say. No. That word holds so much power, yet in that moment I had no ability to say it myself. I couldn't manage to utter it.

Eventually, Aaralyn said it for me. "No," she whispered.

"Aaralyn, she has to complete the dare!" Rachel glared at her and folded her arms.

"No!" Aaralyn said, louder this time. "...I'll get it!" Aaralyn stood from her seat and walked to the kitchen to get the rag.

Deep down, I knew I should have told Rachel no. Shame swept over me. Aaralyn returned to the table.

"Thank you." I mouthed the words to her as she passed my side of the table.

"You're welcome," she whispered and glared at Rachel before she plopped down beside her again. I wondered if the other girls heard her; if they did, there was no sign that they had. A shy smile crossed Aaralyn's face. I felt like I could trust her after all.

Hopefully.

RACHEL

I wanted everyone to believe that I was smart. "Have you been able to find answers to the Chem exam?" I asked. I was on the phone with my best friend, Aaralyn, on my way back home from Klenden.

I stuffed a piece of chocolate candy into my mouth. *Rachel, this is your last piece of chocolate for today,* I told myself. Thankfully, I didn't feel too guilty because I gave most of my candy away to friends at school.

I wanted Aaralyn to find a copy of an exam for me, as she always had. Of course, I knew I shouldn't have been cheating. But I was always at the top of my class, and I wanted it to remain that way until graduation. I wanted people to believe that I was the smartest one at Klenden.

Aaralyn answered with a timid, shaky voice and I rolled my eyes in exasperation. She probably hadn't found the answers yet. "Well, no I haven't yet," she admitted.

Sigh.

Since I lived only minutes away from the Klenden Country Day School campus, I took advantage of the opportunity to get some exercise in by walking home.

I really didn't mind the walk. I was able to feel the crunch of orange and yellow leaves beneath my feet and say hello to some of my friends' parents who ran and biked through the neighborhood.

If I finished my homework early, I usually walked over to the country club and met with a few friends that went to other schools.

Even though school was annoying sometimes, I actually preferred it to being at home. My parents divorced years ago, and I had not been able to get over it.

To make matters worse, my dad decided that he wanted to randomly come back into my life at the beginning of freshman year.

And Mom refused to talk about Dad. Instead, she stressed about providing for both of us without his income. I hardly spoke to either of my parents.

As I approached my house, I desperately wanted an answer from Aaralyn. I didn't want Mom to hear any of our conversation. I knew she wouldn't be happy to hear that her daughter was a cheater. It's not that she didn't have the connections to save me from any consequences of cheating, but she believed in living an honest life.

And besides, she wanted to see all A's on my transcript and eventually an admission letter to a top-ranked college. Cheating was a way to ensure that happened.

Aaralyn continued talking. I wasn't sure what was going on with her. She didn't usually talk that much. "I know someone who might have the answers," she said, "but honestly, Rachel, I just feel like I don't want to do this. I....I don't feel like I want to cheat."

That genuinely surprised me. Aaralyn helped me find exam answers before without a complaint. She just always told me she would, and so I assumed she was fine with it.

She could have told me no, and that would have been okay. She could have told me and I would have found someone else. Sometimes I hardly wanted to cheat.

But... I didn't want *her* to know that. I didn't want *anyone* to know that. I didn't want my classmates to think I was one of the "good girls," and treat me differently if they found out that I didn't like to drink, smoke, or cheat on my tests.

And basically, I didn't want to make everything a complicated mess. So instead, I tried to make Aaralyn feel guilty for not helping me.

"Aaralyn, why are you so *scared* of everything?" I said. I stooped down to tie my boat shoe. I stood and hopped onto my front porch. I quieted my voice to a whisper.

"You always think you're going to get in trouble! But I don't care about getting in trouble, and you shouldn't either! No one's going to find out what we do!"

A harsh pause hindered our conversation. I opened the front door to my house. Aaralyn let out a deep, hard sigh.

"I don't want to argue with you about this anymore," Aaralyn said. "I just believe that there are consequences to our actions, whether someone catches us immediately or not."

Her words echoed in my mind. I wanted them out of my head. *You don't have to tell me about consequences,* I thought. But deep down, I agreed with her. My Dad got caught cheating on my mom, and he left Mom and I struggling.

"Hey, Aaralyn, I'll talk to you later," I told her, and dropped my backpack on the floor of my mom's office. "Just try and find what you can! We can think about consequences later."

Within seconds, I didn't have to worry about Aaralyn because a new idea came to me! I wanted to ask the new girl in our group, Lindsay Alexander, to find the exam answers for us!

Lindsay didn't seem like the type to cheat, but I figured she would be willing to do whatever I told her. And if she did what I told her, then I would still be able to look cool to the people in our grade.

And my desire to appear popular overshadowed my fear that Lindsay wouldn't cheat.

****

Mom sat at the kitchen table in tears. A stack of bills seemed to nearly loom over her head, a typical sight since Dad left. To her left sat an empty bottle of wine; I hated the smell of alcohol. She had let alcohol win. Again.

Mom started drinking after Dad left. And she drank heavily.

To be honest, I was concerned that I was becoming just like her. I drank to fit in with everyone. I drank because I thought it would make me feel better, but it never did.

To Mom's right, a small pan of the brownies I made the previous evening lay empty, devoured. I knew something was up. Mom never ate chocolate like that until Dad left. Same for me.

Mom lifted her head to greet me; tears ran down her cheeks. I wanted more than anything to be at the country club with my friends. Not at home.

"Mom, what happened?" I sank down beside her in my usual spot at the table and she enveloped me in a hug.

Her long brown hair surrounded me, and I hid my face in it for as long as I could muster. She reeked of alcohol; she was drunk.

I didn't want to sit down. I didn't want to talk about feelings with her. I preferred taking action, finding solutions. But I hated seeing my mom cry and I absolutely hated seeing her drunk.

"Yes, Mom?" I said. I wanted to hurry and start the conversation.

She gazed at the empty brownie pan. "I can't believe myself," she said. "I ate the whole thing! Can you believe it? I'm glad my girlfriends aren't here to see this! It's *so* bad!"

I understood, but I just shrugged. Her friends were arrogant anyway. She didn't need their approval. I'm not sure why she thought she did.

"You know how I always said I'd have my business, no matter what?" Mom said. My body tensed up. I knew what was coming. The end of Edenbrooke Draperies.

I couldn't speak; I didn't know what to say. Mom lifted my chin with the tip of her finger.

"I'm giving the company up, Rachel," she slurred. I was right.

I was mad at Dad, and mad that Mom was going through so much because of him. I was mad because a few weeks ago I found out that he-

"I can't find a way to keep the business up!" Mom said. "I want you to stay at Klenden for sure, but things are looking hard for us right now."

I stood and paced. "Mom, have...you heard from him lately?"

Mom shook her head no. I took a deep breath and faced the table. I lifted my head high.

"Are...are you sure this is what you want, Mom? To drop the business?"

"I am so positive! Starting *this* evening!"

I didn't want Mom to drop the business, but I was convinced there was nothing that would change Mom's mind in her drunken state.

"I don't want to talk to Dad anymore," I resolved.

Mom was shocked. "Rachel, that's your da-" she said, but I cut her off.

"Does he care about us? It certainly doesn't seem like it, Mom! So I don't want to see or talk to him!" I started crying.

Mom stood up as if to comfort me and maybe wipe the tears away. But I knew that would make me more upset. And crying never solved anything for me.

Instead, I ran out of the kitchen, up the stairs, and to my room. My room was the one place where I could release all my worries and fears, out of sight from anyone that could judge me.

I closed my door, slid to the floor, and cried. I sobbed like a baby into my pillow that was on the floor. I must have kicked it off the bed in my sleep. I stared at myself in my mirror and cried some more. My whole world was shaken.

I was mad at Dad of course, but I also feared losing our house and transferring schools if my mom could not pay tuition. My whole life was Klenden. It always had been, ever since I started in prekindergarten.

Klenden provided me with resources and access to opportunities that other schools could only dream of offering. My teachers loved me and were gracious with me on my assignments.

My mom was friends with my friends' parents, which allowed me extra access to resources like internships. Even just being around my friends gave me confidence that we would become successful.

I wondered what my friends would think of me if they found out I wasn't one of them anymore. I went on annual spring break trips with them. What was I going to tell them in a few months, that I suddenly couldn't afford to go Europe anymore?

I felt stripped bare. I wondered what would happen if I lost all that my mom worked so hard to give me.

AARALYN

I wanted everyone to believe that I was genuine. But it was hard being genuine at school. At the beginning of freshman year, I wanted to tell Rachel what I thought of her. I wanted to tell her how rude and arrogant she was.

And ever since Rachel asked me to find answers to the upcoming Chemistry exam, I had been stressed out. She made me act like a different person.

I am not generally quiet. I used to love being on camera. I would talk and record videos of myself singing.

I knew what happened to me: my desire to fit in. Over my years at Klenden, my hobbies shifted.

I traded being on camera for holding a camera to take pictures of exam answers for Rachel. I worked on art projects in my house when I didn't have friends to hang out with on the weekends.

In elementary school, many of my classmates were drawn to me and it seemed like I didn't have to worry about making friends. But then a girl named Rachel Edenbrooke stole them away from me by giving them expensive chocolates as she told glamorous stories to them.

They began to like her for what she had and ignored me entirely. Rachel was rich, so I felt that my classmates didn't find me as interesting.

I didn't like being alone, so I decided to befriend Rachel Edenbrooke despite her self-centered behavior.

And even though we were complete opposites, we became "closer" than any other pair of friends at Klenden.

But in order for things to remain that way, I had to listen to Rachel and follow her lead. I couldn't like the boys I wanted to because Rachel would talk to them before I had a chance.

I went from being the spelling bee champion to second-place behind Rachel. I went from giving the best oral presentations to barely raising my hand in class to participate. I let Rachel steal the spotlight.

Rachel took all the awards and attention. People valued her for her hard work, and because Rachel always did so well, I cheered her on too.

It wasn't until eighth grade that I found out Rachel cheated on nearly every assignment. One time I caught her, and she told me that cheating was okay. After all, everyone else was doing it, she said.

To remain on good terms with her, I snuck into classrooms and searched for exam answers for her. Of course, I never used the answers myself...at first. I felt bad about what I was doing and mad at her for getting away with cheating and getting good grades.

Rachel continued to succeed in all of her classes, and I found myself falling behind in nearly every subject. It was then that I resorted to cheating too.

I focused less on my schoolwork and more on what I could do to stay on Rachel's good side, and what I could do to fit in with the other people in my grade.

In eighth grade, some of the people in our grade started drinking and smoking.

I told myself I never wanted to get drawn into any of that, so at parties I pretended to drink. I don't think Rachel, Tanner, Mary, or Brittany were able to tell. I was very careful about it, so no one would call me out on faking.

Secretly, I became jealous of Rachel and how popular she was. *Like, is there anything this girl doesn't have?* I asked myself.

But I still wanted to be Rachel's friend. After all, her parents went through a terrible divorce. I noticed a change in her. The happy girl that once ruled Klenden became angry and withdrawn.

I did whatever she said even more to avoid her anger.

I hated conflict, so I decided the best thing to do was to stay on her good side, so that I would remain in her group.

I didn't want to get kicked out. If I ended up "out", I would be in the same position as Lindsay, struggling to find my place in high school.

I thought Lindsay was nice, and I didn't mind her efforts to join. I just knew that she didn't belong in the group. And to be honest, neither did I.

Over the years, I quietly observed the way Lindsay interacted with others, and decided she wasn't the type to fit in. I guessed that was why Rachel didn't want her to join our group. I wished I could be more like Lindsay.

She didn't fit in with the activities my friends engaged in. She didn't drink, smoke, or do any of the other stuff that "we" did.

I didn't want to be in Rachel's group, but I did. Confusing, right? And the more I didn't speak up to Rachel and stand up for myself, the unhappier I became.

****

During the fourth week of high school, I received a letter telling me to take action on my financial aid forms and visit the financial aid office to turn them in.

I had two missions to complete: turn my payment plan forms in at the Klenden Office of

Admissions and Financial Aid, and find a copy of Chemistry exam answers for Rachel.

At the end of the day, I flew down the emptied hallways of the high school building and rushed down the steps. At the bottom, I adjusted my skirt because it was too short and I'm really tall. It was definitely noticeable.

Klenden required our skirts to be knee length, but Rachel insisted that we wear them short in order to protest the length rule.

And of course, because she is Rachel Edenbrooke, the Dean of Students never spoke a word to us about it. But I didn't really want to break the rules, so I followed dress code when none of my friends were around.

Besides, I was already cheating and that was bad enough.

The Office of Admissions and Financial Aid was its own building, a short distance from the high school building. I slowed my pace and breathed in the smell of fresh, cut grass and waved at the maintenance workers I had seen since I was four years old. It was a pleasant day outside.

Sometimes the stress of fitting in and getting all of my work done made me forget how blessed I was to attend Klenden. It had its faults for sure, just as every school does. But overall, it was a good place.

I entered the doors of the admissions and financial aid building. I yanked my skirt down a bit more, straightened my blue sweater, pulled my knee socks up, and hurriedly tied my hair ribbon around my blonde hair again. I hoped I wasn't late.

The smell of fresh peppermint greeted me at the front desk. There was always a bowl of peppermint drops there.

I grabbed several and checked in with the secretary, Mrs. Fresa.

"Aaralyn Bridgeren?" she said. She stared down at her papers. She looked a little frazzled, perhaps tired from the many admissions tours that came through each afternoon. I hoped she was well.

"Yes, that's me," I said, and stared at the clock on the wall. It was 3:20. My appointment was at 3:30. Hopefully the meeting would be quick so I could go home and work on my latest painting before starting my math homework.

Luckily, I just had to turn my form in, and discuss any additional costs that Klenden added to my student account based on upcoming field trips, like an art museum outing or trip to the local theatre.

Mrs. Fresa directed me to the waiting area. I browsed a few magazines there until it was time for me to meet with the Director of Financial Aid.

Most of the magazines featured the history of Klenden Country Day School. I didn't spend much time looking at them because we had learned all the history backwards and forwards already in class. The last magazine, however, caught my interest because the cover featured my favorite color: bright orange.

While it was not labeled as a "Diversity Magazine," I could clearly tell it was one. I leafed through it, admiring the high resolution of each photo. There were huge smiles on every student's face. Lindsay was in one picture, working on a paper. A blurb of text at the bottom of the photo read:

"Klenden provides a welcoming environment for all of its students."

Wow, I thought. I wondered what Lindsay or any of the other non-white students would think of the magazine. I continued to pour through it until Mrs. Fresa interrupted me.

"Aaralyn!" she called from across the room. "The Director is ready to see you now." I tossed the magazine onto the table on top of the others.

I walked down the hallway behind Mrs. Fresa's desk and stopped at the door of Mr. Hoddard, the Director of Financial Aid.

Just as I reached my arm out to knock on his door, I heard his voice and one other one. I stopped, my arm paused in mid-air.

"Ms. Edenbrooke, don't you worry," Mr. Hoddard said. "We will handle the situation accordingly and you will be considered for a full-tuition scholarship."

Rachel? What is she doing here and why is she being considered for a scholarship? I wondered.

I'm nosy, so I pressed my ear against the door to hear the conversation more clearly.

"Thank you. It means a lot to me," Rachel said in a small voice.

My eyes widened. I thought Rachel's mom paid full tuition!

I thought I could walk away and hide before Rachel saw me. But it was too late! The door opened and Rachel jumped back when she saw me.

"Hi, Aaralyn. How are you?" Mr. Hoddard called from his desk.

"Aaralyn!" Rachel gasped, stepping into the hallway. "How much of that did you hear?"

"Not that much!" I said. I rushed past her and into Mr. Hoddard's office with my form. I accidentally slammed the door behind me.

As I sank into the chair in front of Mr. Hoddard's desk, my thoughts instantly switched to the conversation between Rachel and Mr. Hoddard.

Rachel is going to be considered for a full tuition scholarship?! I couldn't believe it! I didn't want to intrude on her business, but I wondered what had happened.

Rachel's house is big. Her mom is on the Board of Trustees at Klenden. This doesn't make any sense! I couldn't stop thinking about it.

Part of me wanted to feel sorry for Rachel, but most of me didn't. After all of the cheating she had done, arrogance she displayed to teachers and students alike, and her efforts to outdo me, I didn't want to feel sorry for her. *If only people knew that she was faking about still being rich!*

But now Rachel knows that I know. I sighed.

I knew Rachel wasn't buying that I only heard a little bit of the conversation. And I knew she wasn't going to forgive me for hearing it.

LINDSAY

I wanted Rachel to believe that I was a fun person to be around. In October, she invited me and her group to her house to get ready for the Homecoming Dance.

"Are you sure you want to go with this Edenbrooke girl and her friends to this dance?" my mom asked me.

She looked at my dad. "What do you think, Jay?"

Dad grabbed his bagel from the toaster and turned to face me. He had a strange look on his face.

"Uh…yeah, I agree with your Mom wholeheartedly," Dad said. "Are you sure you want to go? And…did you say her name was *Edenbrooke*?"

"Yes, Dad. I am sure! And yeah, her name is Rachel Edenbrooke," I replied.

"And you said Rachel's *mom* would be driving you girls to the dance?" Dad said. "But do you even know what kind of person this Rachel girl is?"

I tried to answer him. "I mean, she seems-"

"I don't want you getting into any trouble at her house, or at this dance," Dad said. His tone was firm.

Mom rolled her eyes. "I wasn't saying anything bad about Rachel *or* her family, Jason. I just don't know them! I want to make sure Lindsay feels comfortable around Rachel and her friends! After all, she doesn't know them that well."

Mom gave me a big hug, one of those tight ones that leave you gasping for air. "Now have you met her parents before?" she asked me.

I shook my head. "No, but I've seen her mom around before," I said.

"As for her dad, I've never met him. Her parents got a divorce a super long time ago! I should be okay, Mom!"

Mom just nodded.

"Dad," I said, "I'll be okay! I know better than to get into trouble!"

Dad didn't respond; he was intensely buttering his bagel. His mind seemed to be elsewhere.

"Lindsay," Mom said. "After this dance, you're going to have to slow things down a bit. You're all over the place! One minute you're writing stories. The next minute you're trying to run around with all these people that you don't know that much about!"

True. I was all over the place, but I'd always been. Maybe all of the books I read were to blame. Books allowed me to travel and learn about other cultures all from the comfort of my cozy couch.

****

I was eager to go over Rachel's house to get ready for Homecoming.

"I'm *so* excited!" Rachel exclaimed. She moved over to make room for me in the car. I climbed in. The car was crowded; Ms. Edenbrooke was driving and the other girls were crammed in the back.

Ms. Edenbrooke didn't seem to share Rachel's enthusiasm. She looked a little sleep deprived.

"Sorry, girls," Ms. Edenbrooke apologized. "I won't be around to take pictures for you because

I have a few business calls to wrap up. Once I finish, I can drive you all to the dance."

Though completely unrelated to what she just said, I recalled my encounter with Rachel from earlier that afternoon. Rachel had pulled me aside in the school hallway and asked me if I could find the answers to our upcoming Chemistry exam.

Aaralyn, who had been at her locker across from us, approached me after Rachel left. She told me that Rachel always asked her to do it, and that she no longer wanted to.

I considered telling Rachel no, and not finding the answers. But I *did* want to become part of her group. And saying no was hard!

"Aaralyn, I need your help!" I pleaded. "Rachel says you know exactly how to find the test answers."

"Okay…just this once," Aaralyn replied. She seemed to feel sorry for me.

We found the answers to the Chem exam lying right on our teacher's desk. It was like our teacher wasn't even *trying* to hide them.

I helped take pictures of the answer key. I knew better than to cheat, but I felt like Rachel would approve so I went along with it. I could only imagine what my parents would say if they knew what I was up to.

As we drove towards the Edenbrooke's house, I wondered if being invited into Rachel's friend group was worth my integrity.

Once Rachel's mom pulled into the driveway, Rachel talked about how many gifts she wanted to receive on her birthday and how expensive her Homecoming dress was. I looked around to see what the other girls were thinking.

As Rachel continued to gloat, Aaralyn rolled her eyes and let out a big sigh. "Here we go again," she muttered under her breath. It seemed like I was the only one that heard her. *Maybe Aaralyn's jealous,* I thought. Rachel *was* wealthy, and many people envied the wealth that she had.

While the other girls rushed through the front door, I pulled Aaralyn aside. "Hey, are you okay?" I asked her.

"I'm fine," was all she said, so I nodded and entered the house. But she didn't seem fine.

It didn't take me long to find out that there was tension between Rachel and Aaralyn.

We sat on the floor of Rachel's room painting our nails with Rachel's nail polish. I sat between Aaralyn and Tanner. Rachel perked up and said, "Lindsay, I meant to tell you how much I *love* your dress!"

I was in the midst of applying color to my nails. I looked up, surprised. I hadn't expected her to say anything to me. Her comment was sooo… random. It threw me off guard. "Thank you, Rachel!" I replied.

She must have taken a look at the dresses we brought over; they were strewn across her bed. I held my hands out and blew on my nails to dry them faster. *Still not dry?* I thought.

"What kind of nail polish *is* this?" I whispered to Aaralyn with a chuckle. "It's probably the same one they sell at the local supermarket!"

"It probably is!" Aaralyn said and rolled her eyes again.

Rachel spoke. "Oh, Aaralyn, what happened with your dress?! Was the original dress you wanted out of stock?"

I looked up. Rachel had a nasty smirk on her face, and she turned to throw Mary, Tanner, and Brittany a look. They smirked at Aaralyn too. *What's going on?* I wondered.

Aaralyn sheepishly said, "Yeah. That's the only dress the store had left in my size, but I kind of like it."

Rachel inspected her nails. "Oh. Okay," she said, her voice rather harsh.

I don't think I like this girl's attitude, I thought. *Maybe I should speak up!* "Your dress is *nice* to me, Aaralyn," I said, challenging Rachel.

I jumped up from the floor and crossed the room to the bed. I lifted Aaralyn's dress up so that the other girls could see it.

It wasn't an ugly dress. It was a beautiful, misty gray with sparkles all over.

"If this looks ugly to you, Rachel, maybe *you* need to take a second look at it!" I said.

Rachel glared. I glared back. Aaralyn mouthed a "Thank you," to me, and the other girls waited for Rachel to respond. She didn't.

I placed the dress back onto the bed with a flourish, then returned to my spot on the floor as if nothing had happened. *Haha! She doesn't know what to say!* I thought.

As if on cue, Rachel walked over to her bed and peered under it as if to look for something.

"Oh," Aaralyn whispered to me in a hushed voice. "This might be awkward."

Rachel returned to our circle holding a bottle of wine and several cups. I picked with my bracelet. *Lindsay, you need to be COURAGEOUS*, I told myself.

"It's party time!" Rachel exclaimed, holding the bottle high.

Tanner, Mary, and Brittany stood up to grab cups. Rachel filled them with the red-colored liquid. I reluctantly took a cup when Rachel handed one to me.

I had never tasted a drop of alcohol in my life, and I hadn't planned to that evening. But I didn't want Rachel to call me out the way she had with Aaralyn.

Aaralyn leaned over to whisper into my ear. "I just pretend to drink it," she said. "Then when no one's looking I go to her bathroom and pour it down the sink." She shrugged and pretended to take a sip from her cup.

I held my cup with both hands, unsure of what to do. I knew the *right* thing to do. But why was it so hard to just tell Rachel I didn't want to drink?

I knew I shouldn't have cheated for Rachel, so why didn't I just tell her I didn't want to? Why didn't I tell her I didn't want to get the rag at lunch on the first day? Why did I--?

"Why do you pretend?" I whispered to Aaralyn. "Why not just tell her you don't drink?"

I wanted to hear her answer because maybe we were both just scared of the same thing: rejection.

Aaralyn made sure none of the other girls were paying attention. They weren't; they were too busy pouring more drinks. "I don't want them to know. I guess I'm just scared of not having friends," she admitted.

She spoke again. "Lindsay, I don't want to get kicked out the grou-"

"The clique," I finished for her, interrupting. I wanted to make myself admit the truth and wanted her to see it too. "That's what it is."

Aaralyn gave a quick nod and pretended to take another sip of her drink.

"Is this all really worth it?" I asked her. "The pretending to drink? The fake smiles? All of it?"

Aaralyn didn't answer me, so I guessed she thought it was worth it.

It was ironic because I thought it was worth it too…at first, or else I would have stayed home instead of going to Homecoming.

I didn't mean to make our conservation super deep, but I suddenly wondered what we had become. How desperate were we?

I continued talking. "I understand that it feels good to fit in, Aaralyn, but what does it matter if you lose who you are along the way?" Aaralyn didn't answer me.

I peered down at the alcohol in my cup. *This isn't me*, I thought. No matter what, I had to be myself. Never had I ever imagined myself coming so close to drinking.

Aaralyn pulled out her phone and texted someone.

I made my way to the bathroom to pour out the alcohol in my cup.

After a while, Rachel, Mary, Tanner, and Brittany centered their attention on me and Aaralyn.

"Hey, Aaralyn!" Rachel yelled. Her voice was super loud. "Who are you texting? Hopefully not Max, because I told you he would never go for you!" She snickered and the other girls laughed.

As if Rachel's first outburst wasn't enough, she stood up on her bed and said, "You wanna know the truth? He doesn't like boring girls, and he **never** will!"

Aaralyn's green eyes filled with tears. Even though Rachel's comments weren't directed at me, I felt hurt by them; they hurt Aaralyn.

I didn't like Rachel's behavior, so I decided to be courageous again.

"Wait a minute, Rachel!" I said as I stood from the floor. Rachel had gone too far! "How could you say that?"

I was confused because I thought Aaralyn and Rachel were best friends. *What happened?* I wondered.

Before Rachel could respond, Aaralyn ran out of the room. I followed after her. I wasn't sure what had caused the friction between the two of them, and I wanted to figure out what was going on.

Right then and there, I decided that being in Rachel's group wasn't worth it.

I had more self-respect than that.

I ran through the hall and down the stairs to help the one friend I *did* have.

AARALYN

I wanted everyone to believe that I was better than Rachel. In art class one December afternoon, my focus should have been solely on painting. But I couldn't help but think back to the night of the Homecoming dance a few weeks before.

****

The night of the dance, I ran into Rachel's kitchen and cried. Lindsay came to check on me, and we had a powerful discussion about remaining true to ourselves.

I really like conversations like that, because they help bring me back to the kind of person I really hope to be.

And I discovered how much I loved hanging around Lindsay, and wished we had become friends earlier. If only I hadn't spent so much time trying to fit in.

During the dance, I stayed on the sidelines with Lindsay and tried to hold back tears. I didn't even have the courage to go over to my crush, Max, and speak to him. I feared that Rachel would have said something to get on my nerves. I also feared that she would have started a fight because I knew about her true financial situation. It wasn't my fault that I heard it, but I knew she would have blamed me all the same.

I was sure Rachel was mean to me because she was angry, angry because her reputation as the smartest and richest girl was at stake. She was afraid I would tell other people, just because she didn't want her reputation "ruined." I knew she was drunk when she lashed out at me, but that didn't excuse her behavior. I felt like I couldn't muster up the courage to say something back when she embarrassed me in front of the others.

Instead, I kept quiet. I never allowed myself to truly deal with the problem at hand by telling her off.

I really wanted people to see how fake and mean she was. I thought that then more people would have wanted to be friends with me.

****

I set my paintbrush to the side, lifted my canvas up, and tilted my head back to admire my masterpiece: a lighthouse on the ocean. The white of the lighthouse contrasted perfectly with the blues and purples I had chosen for the waves.

I had never been to Maine, but I read a travel book about the state. It was filled with historical facts, pictures, and recipes.

One picture that caught my eye featured a lighthouse, and so I decided to paint it during my art class.

"Aaralyn! Aaralyn!" Mrs. Casava called. I jumped. My teacher caught me daydreaming again.

She stood with her arms folded, a tight smile on her face. There was no need for me to fear, however, because that was simply the look she gave to show she approved of my work.

"Your painting is beautiful!" She told the class to look at it.

"That's pretty good," one of the boys said.

"What's the location of the painting?" one of the girls asked.

"Maine," I said. "I based it off a photo of a lighthouse there that I really like."

After everyone admired it, it was time to leave class for the day and return to my locker.

****

I looked both ways before I darted down the hallway. I couldn't wait to get home. That night, Mom and Dad planned to make a special dinner, and I wanted to help them cook for once. I figured it was the best I could do to help around the house, since my homework rendered me unavailable most of the time.

I didn't want to think about Rachel or my work. But just before I could manage to grab my backpack and leave, Rachel and the girls entered the hallway. I really didn't want to see any of them.

Ever since the dance I felt uncomfortable around them. I stopped eating with them and speaking to them, but that didn't make running into them any less awkward. And because Klenden was so small, I was destined to run into them multiple times a day.

"Aaralyn!" Lindsay called me. She ran up beside me. She tugged my arm. "Don't even look at them! They just want to make a scene!"

Lindsay looked happier than I had seen her in a long time. Her face glowed. I knew my face sure wasn't glowing. I was also pretty sure my hair ribbon had either fallen out or was about to fall out of my hair. I never tied it in good enough.

"I....I just don't like running into Rachel." I sighed. "Things are just too awkward now, and I'm always afraid she'll say something to me."

Lindsay gave a slight smile. "Have you considered that she might just want to come up and apologize?" I didn't smile back.

Lindsay tried again to make me feel better. "*You* shouldn't be the one hiding," she said. She placed a hand on her hip. "*Rachel* was wrong."

I nodded, but Lindsay still didn't seem to get how uncomfortable the situation was. I had been around Rachel for years. Not talking to her felt weird; other than Lindsay, I had no one else to be around.

I didn't even wear my blue sweater anymore, and Rachel and the girls used every opportunity they could to tease me about it.

"Yeah, she *was* wrong," I agreed. "But the reason why Rachel said anything to me about my dress is because she's mad at me! She's mad because I discovered how *fake* she is! And she doesn't want anyone else to see it!" I started to cry.

Lindsay sank to the floor and sat against the lockers behind us. Letting out a deep breath, I plopped down to the floor beside her.

"Aaralyn, you have to stop letting Rachel determine whether or not you are happy!" she said.

I stared at Lindsay; maybe she *did* understand how I felt about losing Rachel as a friend. After all, Lindsay had gone longer than I had with no friends. Maybe I had been so busy focusing on myself that I hadn't even noticed that other people didn't fit in too.

Lindsay used to look anxious and afraid around Rachel and the other girls in the group. Over the past month, however, I noticed a change in her. She looked more self-confident.

"Aaralyn, at least *you* know why Rachel is mad at you! I don't even know why Rachel doesn't like me!" Lindsay said. "For all I know, there could be no reason at all! I've spent years analyzing and questioning everyone's motives. I wondered why people didn't like me, and tried to make them accept me. Until..." Here she stopped, and I desperately wanted to know what she was going to say.

"Until what?" I asked.

"Until I learned that I would never be able to find answers to *all* my questions. And that I can't wear myself out anymore trying to figure everything out."

I raised my eyebrows. After so many years seeking and maintaining Rachel's approval, I became so used to analyzing her every action and motive. Apparently Lindsay had done that too.

I considered telling Lindsay that I believed Rachel didn't want her in the group because she didn't drink or smoke, but I decided against it; Lindsay really didn't seem to care anymore.

"Maybe one day we'll be able to speak to Rachel and figure out why she acts the way she does," Lindsay said. We stood from the floor.

I think Lindsay said a bit more, but I wasn't paying attention at that point because Rachel, Tanner, Mary, and Brittany walked towards us wearing those annoying blue sweaters.

"Don't you just *love* these sweaters!" Tanner bragged in a loud, animated voice.

"I love how we *all* match!" Brittany added. "I'm glad *all of us* are wearing them!"

Rachel didn't say a word. Instead, she led them to the right side of the hallway where Lindsay and I stood. They pretended as if they were going to walk right into us, and before they did, they scooted over towards the middle of the hallway. They disappeared down the end of the hall.

My heart sank. I couldn't be like Lindsay; she was confident and didn't care what they thought. I had been around those girls nearly all my life. It was hard for me not to care.

"Don't worry about them," Lindsay tried to encourage me, but I was barely listening. I felt hurt. "We could start our own sweater club! The school store sells them in other colors too!" She chuckled at the idea.

I didn't respond. Instead, I peered around the hallway and noticed that there were flyers on every locker. Every locker but *mine*.

Actually, every locker except mine and Lindsay's.

Curiosity got the best of me; I wandered over to the locker to see what the flyers said. Lindsay followed me.

I nervously adjusted my skirt. "You're invited to Rachel's 15th birthday party," Lindsay read one of the flyers aloud.

I nearly burst into tears. I felt angry again. Lindsay turned and faced me.

"It's going to suck!" she said, shaking her head. "I'm *glad* we're not going!"

For years, I put my happiness aside to do everything I could for Rachel. I stole answers to exams and pretended to be innocent.

I put myself in uncomfortable situations, and sat through many lunches with her that would have been better spent alone. And all for what?

"I feel bad for Rachel," Lindsay said.

"Why?' I asked.

"Maybe she has personal problems that we don't know about," she said.

Hmm, I know of one in particular, I thought. But I *did* want to forgive Rachel and maybe even befriend her again.

"Hey, how about we show up at her party?" I asked.

"For what?" Lindsay said. "She didn't invite us."

"Yeah," I said, "but I think that going would be the perfect opportunity to speak to her about what happened during Homecoming. I want to see things from her point of view."

Lindsay smiled and nodded. "Sure. I'll go too," she said. "Maybe we'll both find out why Rachel has acted the way she has."

RACHEL

I wanted everyone to believe that I was ready for the party. It was January 5th, my birthday. *My name is Rachel Edenbrook*, I told myself. *I am 15 years old now, and I am* **going** *to be ready for this party*. I looked into the huge mirror in my bedroom. I looked like a mess.

My curls were ruined because I was on my bed so long crying into my pillow. I hadn't even put my hair into a bun like I usually did. But I had to pull myself together and become the girl everyone thought I was at school. Sigh.

Was I a perfectionist? Hardly, but I wanted to throw a perfect birthday party that year so none of my classmates would suspect things had changed for Mom and I.

I feared that Aaralyn mentioned something about my financial situation to someone.

I would have hardly blamed her if she had. After all, I lashed out at her before Homecoming when I was drunk. After I had promised myself I would never get drunk like my mom.

A few days before my birthday, Mom left town to try and save what remained of Edenbrooke Draperies. The headquarters were in Chicago, so I didn't expect her to be back until after the party.

While I was exuberant because she wouldn't be around to ruin the party, my joy was ephemeral.

Dad texted me early that morning and said he would stop by before the party to wish me a happy birthday. Was I happy to hear that news? No.

After all, I barely saw him as it was. Not only was I mad at him for leaving me with the shameful task of asking for a full-tuition scholarship at Klenden, but I was also mad because he also did something that completely changed my perception of him.

I found out a week before the start of freshman year.

****

In early August, I sat at my desk and tried to call Dad on my phone several times. I brought a couple of chocolate chip cookies I baked with me, nibbling on them here and there for stress relief.

He didn't answer my calls. My only other option was to look for his work number in his old office and try that one.

I rummaged around the drawers, desperately searching for a number to contact him with. Did he not care that I hadn't talked to him or seen him in months?

I yanked open the last drawer. A solitary photo was inside.

'2005,' the back of the picture read. I turned it over and gasped once I had looked at it; I placed my hand to my mouth. I couldn't do anything but stare, shocked.

There in the photo was my dad, a black woman with light brown hair, and a little black girl that looked kind of like me.

It felt like they were staring back at me, smiling at me. Scratch that. They smirked at me. I was appalled.

The woman had her arm around Dad, *my* Dad! The woman and the little girl stole my Dad!

I looked closely at the girl, holding the photo up to the desk lamp in the office. *Dad must have had a little girl the same time he had me!* I realized. I was disgusted. We looked about the same age!

That's when it hit me.

"No. Freaking. Way!" I yelled. "Wait a minute! Why that little...that *is* her!"

Tears poured down my cheeks. *I can't believe this!* I thought.

I ripped the photo to shreds and tossed it in the trash can beside me.

I wasn't sorry I destroyed it, and I no longer wanted to call my Dad again.

The girl in the photo was Lindsay Alexander! Suddenly, everything made sense. Lindsay's last name was Alexander. And mine was supposed to be since my Dad's last name is Alexander.

My mom chose to take her anger out on my Dad by changing my last name to her maiden name.

All along, I had thought it odd that Lindsay and I shared the same last name and looked a tiny bit alike, but I never thought about it too much.

Why hadn't he told me? Was it because he was ashamed?

I marched out of the office, ran up the staircase, and down the long hall. I stormed into my room and landed onto my soft, frilly bed. As far as I was concerned, my world had been destroyed and I didn't want to see my dad ever again.

****

My name is Rachel Edenbrooke, and I have a party to host. I stood at the mirror and tried again to calm down. I took a few, deep breaths and wished more than anything that Dad wouldn't come to the party.

I tried to change my mood and smile. I tried to put on a facade once more. I had become so accustomed to acting at Klenden. I adjusted my dark curls on my shoulders and smiled. I stood up straight, with my shoulders back.

"My name is Rachel Edenbrooke," I began again slowly, my voice shaky. "I am 15 years old today, and I am *ready* for this party."

Just then, I heard my mom enter the house.

She was home early from Chicago?!

LINDSAY

I wanted Aaralyn to know that she didn't **have** to be friends with Rachel. And I hoped that after talking to Rachel at the party, Aaralyn would understand that she would be better off avoiding her.

Sometimes I considered writing a book about my life. I mean, doesn't everyone at some point? That particular day, the day of Rachel's party, my life went from ordinary to brand new in a matter of hours and I found that I *really* had something to write about.

Dad was adamant that Mom take me to Rachel's house for the party. Mom explained that she had errands to run downtown and argued that Dad already promised to take me, so Dad sulked a bit on the drive to Rachel's.

Naturally, I was a Daddy's girl from the start. He was always there for me from what I could remember. I believe I got my personality from him. Looks? No. His skin is slightly lighter than my dark brown complexion.

In fact, Dad almost looks white.

"Dad, you okay?" I asked him in the car. He wasn't normally so quiet.

He didn't answer. Instead, he turned the volume up on the radio. His fingers trembled at the knob.

"Dad?" I repeated, louder this time to drown out the sound of the music.

"Yes, Lindsay?" he said, turning to look at me for the first time.

"Are you okay? You're acting strange today." I folded my arms.

It took him a moment to answer. Finally, he said, "Yes, Lindsay. I'm okay. It's just that there's something I want you to know and *need* you to know. But it's going to be hard for me to talk about it. In fact, I was almost going to put it off...and not mention it today."

We entered Rachel's neighborhood. Dad tightened his grip on the steering wheel. *What is going on?* I wondered. *What does he need to tell me?*

Dad stopped the car down the street from Rachel's house.

"Now, I'll let you out right here, and you can walk the rest of the way," Dad said.

"Wait...why?" I asked, and I know he answered but I didn't hear him. I checked my phone instead because Aaralyn had just texted me.

She was waiting at Rachel's house, so I said bye to my dad and walked the rest of the way.

Aaralyn stood just outside the front door on the porch.

"Has Rachel seen you yet?" I asked. Aaralyn shook her head no; she looked scared.

I wanted to tell her again not to worry about Rachel, and to not worry about being part of Rachel's clique.

But being accepted was rooted so deeply in her that it was almost as if Aaralyn couldn't accept anything less than being part of the clique, even if it meant getting mistreated.

"Lindsay! Aaralyn! Why are you here?" Rachel said. We turned to see Rachel standing inside the house, scowling through the screen door.

I looked at Aaralyn. She seemed too scared to say a word.

"We want to talk to you about something," I said. "I know it's not the best time, but we both think it's important."

Rachel's eyes widened; she looked alarmed. "Wait....do you...*know*, Lindsay? Aaralyn, do you know *too*?" she stammered. Her emphasis on the word *know* was puzzling. What did she mean?

Before I could ask what she thought we knew, Rachel's mom bustled over to the foyer and peered out the door. "Hi, girls," she interrupted. I could tell she was troubled, but she tried her best to disguise it.

Her smile was too wide, her eyes distracted. "Thanks for coming! Rachel and I are *so* glad you are here."

Just as Ms. Edenbrooke finished her greeting, Rachel's eyes followed her mom's gaze. They stared at a man coming down the street. Aaralyn and I turned and watched from the porch.

It was probably best that I was the last to see. I would have probably passed out if I had seen him any earlier.

It was Dad.

He continued his almost tortoise-like pace as he made his way towards the house, his car parked right where he dropped me off.

"Dad?" Rachel and I exclaimed.

We looked at each other. I was so confused. *Why is she calling him Dad too?* I wondered.

Aaralyn looked just as confused as I felt.

"Jay?" Ms. Edenbrooke said. *Rachel's mom knows my dad? How does she know him?* I wanted answers.

Rachel crossed her arms and shifted her gaze to the floor. *Could it be that...Rachel and I have the same Dad?*

"Wait. What?!" I exclaimed. "What's going on here?"

No one answered me, so I waited until Dad arrived at the porch.

****

My father, Jay Alexander, had two families. My father, Jay Alexander, was also Rachel's Dad. The evening of Rachel's birthday party, we found out that Dad and Rachel's mom dated in graduate school. Rachel's mom became pregnant right before graduation.

Dad's parents and Ms. Edenbrooke's parents made them get married. So they did, and Rachel was born shortly after the wedding.

And it turns out things weren't so straightforward. Mom was a close friend of Dad's throughout graduate school; he was in love with her and she with him. And Mom, not knowing about the arranged marriage Dad had to Rachel's mom, became pregnant with me.

Unfortunately, this conflict eventually led to a divorce between my Dad and Ms. Edenbrooke after she had discovered Dad would check on Mom and I at our place because he missed us.

He eventually married my mom long before I could remember any details from my childhood, and Ms. Edenbrooke changed Rachel's last name to match hers.

Rachel and I went to the same school, but Dad kept that a secret. Dad, ashamed of what occurred years ago, kept his distance to ensure we didn't find out the truth until he was ready to tell us.

While Ms. Edenbrooke worked on the Board of Trustees, he stayed in the shadows.

He worked hard at his job so that both of us could attend Klenden. But by the end of our 8th grade year, he couldn't afford Klenden for both us of us anymore. He said he didn't mean to leave Rachel and her mom out in the cold, but that he felt he had no other choice.

After all, he *was* married to my mom and wanted to ensure I had a good life too. Rachel's Mom was rich until her business failed a few months ago. My Mom, on the other hand, was a stay at home mom. So his priority was with Mom and I.

And neither Rachel or I knew until the day of Rachel's 15th birthday party, or so I thought. Dad excused himself after telling Rachel happy birthday. I didn't want to speak to him at the time. Rachel didn't say anything, and Aaralyn pretended to look around the room. It was like time froze.

The family "reunion" continued inside Ms. Edenbrooke's office. Rachel stood in a corner of the room. The entire time she refused to sit; instead, she paced.

Rachel admitted that she found the picture of Dad, Mom, and I right before the start of freshman year.

She had known that we were half-sisters since the *beginning* of the year!

"Mom, why didn't you say anything?" Rachel asked, a hint of sternness to her voice. "You knew this whole time!"

"Say what? I just knew that Jay was out of our lives!" Ms. Edenbrooke said. "I knew about your dad's marriage, but I didn't know that you had a half-sister!"

Rachel looked confused and tired.

Ms. Edenbrooke stood and pushed her chair in at the desk, excusing herself. "I'll... I'll check on the guests. After all, there is a party going on," she said. "I'll expect the three of you girls have a lot to talk about." She left the office.

"This...is really crazy," Aaralyn stammered. "Um, I don't know what else to say. Should...I go?" I was about to tell her to stay, but Rachel jumped in. "No, Aaralyn. Stay. I have some apologies to make," she said.

Maybe Rachel, my sister, didn't hate me.

RACHEL

I wanted everyone to believe that I was perfect. But man, I had totally messed up in keeping everything to myself. I had to deal with the consequences of my actions. Aaralyn was definitely right about consequences.

I took a deep breath. Lindsay and Aaralyn waited for me to speak. I moved from my place in the corner and sat in the chair Mom had just left. I tried to toughen up and appear to be calm. But I couldn't keep tears from flowing.

Aaralyn looked helpless, as if she didn't know what to do. Lindsay stood and pat my shoulder, which made me cry harder. After how I had treated her, I didn't know why she was comforting me.

"I'll try to keep this short," I said slowly. "There's some things I'd like to admit. Lindsay, it's not that I didn't like you! I was jealous because Dad lives with you and your mom, and I apologize. I felt like my world fell apart when he left.

"I didn't have to worry about financial aid before. In fact, I hadn't stepped foot into the financial aid office until this year."

Lindsay nodded, as if she accepted my apology. "It's okay, Rachel," she said. "I thought you hated me or something! After all, I didn't know the situation about our Dad until today."

Aaralyn stared down at the floor.

"Aaralyn," I continued. "I apologize for treating you the way I did. I got mad at you that day when you ran into me at the financial aid office. But it wasn't really *you* I was angry at. I was mad because I thought you might have thought I was poor and because I thought you would tell the other girls! And...I was afraid."

"Afraid? Wow!" Aaralyn said. She crossed her arms. "Rachel, what did *you* of all people have to be afraid of at Klenden?"

"I was afraid of not having friends," I sighed. "Ever since I arrived at Klenden, I felt like I wouldn't fit in if people knew I'm black."

This year, I wondered what everyone would think if they knew my financial situation and that my life isn't as glamorous as it used to be.

"I even started drinking not too long ago too. I first tried alcohol thinking I would just try it once.

But it turned into a habit, and because I felt bad about my own drinking, I made fun of people who don't drink. The main thing I tried to do was pretend the divorce didn't happen, and pretended that I was still rich."

Aaralyn nodded slowly, as if she realized she was wrong too.

"Oh," Aaralyn admitted. "I apologize too, because I thought you tried so hard to impress people because you thought you were better than everyone, including me!

"And when I saw you that one day at the Office of Admissions and Financial Aid, I uh...thought you were lying to everyone about your life."

I felt horrible. My personal problems made me hurt other people along the way. And I didn't even care at the time. I had made everything about me.

The silence that filled the room was awkward, and it seemed like Lindsay was trying to come up with something to say. She did.

"Well, I'm glad we all know the truth now," she said. "I forgive you, Rachel. Forgiveness has always been so hard. When people wrong me,

it's easy to just think about myself and how bad

they hurt me. But others have forgiven me for

things I have done, so I know that I can

forgive."

I heard what Lindsay said, but I couldn't

bring myself to forgive Dad.

I was still bitter. Dad admitted the truth to us

that day, and I was glad he did. But I was still

mad at him for the years of lying and hiding he

did. I was angry because of the financial situation

he left Mom and I in.

But keeping all of that negativity in me didn't

resolve my hurt feelings; instead, it made me feel

worse.

I knew I *needed* to forgive our Dad. I didn't know how or when, but I knew in my heart of hearts that it was the right thing to do.

"Lindsay, you're right. I need to forgive Dad," I said. "But I can't."

"I know it won't be easy," Lindsay said. "It'll take some time. But once you see that you have to in order to feel better, you'll recognize it's worth it."

Aaralyn didn't speak, but I could tell she was thinking about what Lindsay had said as well. I figured it was going to be hard for her to forgive me too.

The three of us left the office and joined the guests wandering around the house.

I gazed at my guests. All from Klenden. These were the people I tried to impress since I was four years old.

Some of their parents were also business owners. Some were doctors and lawyers. Most were not on financial aid like I was. But, did money really matter that much after all? I had chased the applause of people, and it led me to do things I wouldn't have dreamed of doing previously.

I realized that our choices don't just affect us; they affect other people. My dad probably didn't realize how much his actions harmed his daughters.

I decided to chase a good reputation, and had my friends cheating for me so that I could get better grades.

My mom drank heavily, unaware that her daughter was being influenced by her decisions.

As I stood against the living room wall watching people go to and fro, I learned that we all have the ability to impact lives, and I was sure that I wanted to impact others' lives for the better.

Maybe Klenden wasn't really everything. I had built it up and praised myself for all of the things I could do because of the opportunities Klenden gave me.

I did that all so that no one could see that I came from a broken home, and that I didn't have two parents to spend time with.

AARALYN

I want everyone to believe that the quality of your friends is more important than the *quantity* of them.

After talking to Rachel, I discovered how wrong my thinking had been. I didn't consider that Rachel had something difficult going on in her life.

I know that doesn't excuse her behavior, but it gave me something to think about for sure. Lindsay was right. I didn't need to spend so much time worrying about what Rachel and the other girls thought of me.

I decided that even if I had one good friend all of my life, that was better than being around a group of girls that didn't care about me.

"Happy Birthday, Lindsay!" I cheered, my braids swinging as I skipped alongside my friend down the school hallway.

It was February and school was over for the day. Also, because of an upcoming blizzard, Klenden decided to close for the next few days.

I had to give Lindsay her birthday presents before the break.

I felt joyful for once. An incredible burden was lifted off my shoulders after Rachel talked to us at the party.

It turns out that Rachel didn't hate me. There were things that I had seen completely wrong, and it was good to know that the three of us could move forward on much different terms.

After Lindsay showed me her 'COURAGEOUS' bracelet, I looked for a similar one. I finally found one at a gift shop near my house.

My new bracelet bounced up and down on my wrist as I skipped down the hallway.

Lindsay smoothed her matching braids down and threw her winter hat and snow boots on. I reached into the bottom of my locker, grabbed a shiny, gray gift bag and handed it to Lindsay.

I gave her a card I decorated, a notebook, and frosted cookies from the bakery just outside our school campus. "Wow!" she cried. "Thanks Aaralyn!"

She opened the cookie package and took one out to eat.

Her eyes wandered towards the end of the hall, where Rachel, Brittany, Mary, and Tanner stood together, laughing. When Rachel saw Lindsay, she waved politely and Lindsay waved back.

It was nice to see that the two sisters got along. At first, things were awkward for everyone. Their Dad still stayed with Lindsay and her Mom, and Rachel stayed with her Mom.

We didn't know what would happen next, but I hoped that Rachel would find a way to spend more time with their Dad.

A large group of our classmates surrounded Rachel and they laughed and talked together. For a minute I considered what it would be like to join Rachel's group again.

"Do you ever miss being in Rachel's clique?" Lindsay asked, as if she read my mind. I always felt that Lindsay could read my mind sometimes. I cringed. I still wasn't too fond of the word "clique."

"I used to," I admitted. "But now, I'm kind of glad I'm not in it. I've had time to enjoy my favorite things, like painting."

Lindsay took a look at the card I gave her. A painting of us with matching braids was on the front, and a lighthouse was on the inside pages. It was similar to the one I painted for my art class.

"This is beautiful, Aaralyn," Lindsay said. "You could definitely do something big with this!"

"Thanks," I replied. "I used to hold back a little with my art. Rachel and I used to be in the same art classes, and I didn't want her to get mad when the teacher praised my work instead of hers."

I stopped talking, laughing at how stupid that sounded. That was back when fear ruled my life.

"What about you, Lindsay?" I asked. "Do you miss being in her group?"

"It's weird," Lindsay said. "I feel like Rachel and I should talk a little more. After all, we are sisters, but I kind of like the way things are now. We text each other sometimes and keep it at that. I believe when we're ready, things will change. But for now, it is what it is."

I liked her perspective. She wasn't desperate for anything else.

"Aaralyn, I think you have just become *Uncliqueable!*" Lindsay cheered. She jumped up and down, her braids bouncing against her back.

Uncliqueable? "Uncliqueable?!" I laughed. "What does that mean?"

"It means that you are unable to be "cliqued," she said. "It means that you are courageous. And it means that you are so confident in yourself that you are not willing to throw away who you are in order to become like someone else."

She held out her wrist, showing me her COURAGEOUS bracelet.

I held out my wrist too, revealing my new bracelet Lindsay had not seen. It read, 'CONFIDENT.'

"Uncliqueable is an awesome word, Lindsay," I said, trying to sound just as confident. "I want to be Uncliqueable too! I won't let fear make me change myself for anyone else!"

EPILOGUE

LINDSAY

I wanted to believe that I wouldn't get in trouble. But I did. One day in the high school hallway, I heard the voice of a man I never had too much interaction with and didn't plan to have any interaction with. The Dean of Students.

"Lindsay Alexander! Aaralyn Bridgeren!" he called; his voice echoed off the ancient walls of the high school.

Aaralyn and I froze in place; her eyes were wide and my teeth chattered. "Oh, no!" we exclaimed. We instantly knew why the Dean of Students was there.

The Dean of Students, Mr. Redd, didn't have the most pleasant disposition, and he struck fear into the heart of every high school student at Klenden. His presence doubled the fear of students on any financial aid.

More was at stake for financial aid kids because our parents didn't have any influence at Klenden, and thus our financial aid was on the line if we got in trouble.

He reached us and folded his arms. "Aaralyn, Lindsay, could I see both of you in my office? There's been an episode of cheating in the freshman chemistry class, and I've received information that both of you were involved."

I was so willing to fit in that I did something wrong, and that day I faced the consequences of my actions.

Moments before my meeting with both the Dean and the Director of Financial Aid, I spotted a picture of myself in a "diversity" magazine spread on the coffee table in the admissions office.

For some reason, seeing my face on a school magazine made me even more nervous for the punishment I would receive.

That day was not the highlight of my high school experience. I guess that goes to show that desiring something too much can lead to trouble. My desire to be more popular and to fit in with a group of girls that were a bad influence on me lead me to make bad choices.

That afternoon, waiting in the pickup circle for my Mom, I felt horrible. I didn't want to face my parents and tell them what I did.

I hardly ever got in trouble, so when my parents found out I had to not only meet with the Dean of Students, but also the Director of Financial Aid, I knew they would flip.

Suddenly, as if by divine intervention, I received an email from the Klenden Country Day School Office of Admissions and Financial Aid telling me that I would remain on financial aid.

****

I want everyone to believe that the circumstances you find yourself in now don't have to always be. At the start of freshman year, I was convinced that I needed to put more effort into finding friends or else things would never change.

And even though I found my sister and best friend through my efforts, I am now positive that I would have found friends at some point in my life.

Of course, everyone wants friends, but I learned that God wanted to give me the very best. I spent years chasing groups of people that had nothing good to offer me, and was hurt when they didn't accept me.

Now I no longer fear not fitting in. If I don't make friends in a certain situation, then the people in that situation must not have been for me.

I was outside Klenden Country Day School one morning in March. Mom just dropped me off and I was ready for an exciting day of learning ahead.

Rachel flew towards me with a large bag in her hands, the emblem of our school displayed on the sides. "Lindsay, wait up!"

She was panting, so I slowed my pace and waited for her to catch up to me. Her hair fell out of its usual bun, and her curls bounced on her shoulders.

As if on cue, Aaralyn hurried towards me from the other direction. Because she wasn't carrying a bag, she reached me first. "Hey, Lindsay!" she cried.

Rachel arrived and sat her bag on the sidewalk outside the high school entrance. "Lindsay! I got something for you. I've been meaning to give it to you for a long time," she said.

I was puzzled. What could Rachel possibly fix about our life situation by handing me a gift?

****

Though it had been months since we learned that we were sisters, things were still awkward between us.

I was glad to hear that Rachel no longer bossed her other friends around. In fact, she tried her hardest to focus less on herself and more on other people. Aaralyn and I remained good friends, of course, but Rachel was more of a good acquaintance.

Rachel and I had decided it would be best for us to talk, but go our separate ways. She became friendlier and even asked if she could come with

Mom and I to our church potluck in May. It turns out she likes to bake like I do and offered to bring brownies.

I didn't use to know why I ended up at Klenden Country Day School or why I went without friends most of my time there, but I knew that God must have had a purpose behind it.

Now I know why. I found my sister, and in my sister I have found a new friend. I also found my friend, Aaralyn, and inspired her to enjoy the sweetness of being Uncliqueable.

I got to thinking that perhaps our experiences not only mold and shape us, but also allow us to encourage other people going through similar things.

I realized that my hobbies, reading and writing, could be used to inspire other people to become Uncliqueable too. And I realized for sure that I wanted to write a book.

****

I reached down into Rachel's bag to see what the present was, and Aaralyn stepped closer to us to peek in. A folded navy blue sweater was inside. I gasped in surprise. "A sweater?" I said, and Rachel nodded.

"All yours," she said, in a quieter voice than usual. "You never got a sweater. I thought maybe you wanted one, so here you go."

I lifted it out of the bag, and gently traced the Klenden emblem on it with my fingertip. A few months ago, the sweaters meant much more to me. They symbolized popularity and acceptance. I wanted one at the time.

But standing outside, with my sister on my left and my best friend on my right, I realized the sweater didn't carry the same meaning for me that it once did.

I did, however, appreciate my sister's kind gesture. "Thank you," I said, my voice soft. Rachel nodded. I hoped she wasn't too upset because I wasn't excited, but if she was, there was no indication of it on her face.

After Rachel walked into the building, Aaralyn gave me a reassuring smile. I think she could tell I didn't truly want it.

"It *is* a nice sweater though, Lindsay. I would keep it," she said encouragingly. "It was nice of your sister to get it for you."

I decided she was right.

"Just as the Lord has forgiven you, so you must also forgive," (Colossians 3:13)

Made in the USA
Lexington, KY
03 July 2018